MW00906267

TJ and the
Quiz Kids

ORCA
YOUNG
READERS

TJ and the

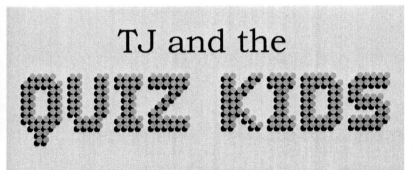

Hazel
Hutchins

ORCA BOOK PUBLISHERS

Copyright © 2007 Hazel Hutchins

All rights reserved. No part of this publication may be reproduced or transmitted
in any form or by any means, electronic or mechanical, including photocopying,
recording or by any information storage and retrieval system now known or to be
invented, without permission in writing from the publisher.

Library and Archives Canada Cataloguing in Publication

Hutchins, H. J. (Hazel J.)
TJ and the quiz kids / written by Hazel Hutchins.

(Orca young readers)
ISBN 978-1-55143-731-6

I. Title. II. Series.

PS8565.U826T328 2007   jC813'.54   C2007-903647-3

First published in the United States in 2007
Library of Congress Control Number: 2007929833

Summary: When master fact-gatherers TJ and Seymour are asked to join
the school *Quiz Kids* team, TJ once again downplays his own abilities.

Free teachers' guide available at www.orcabook.com

Orca Book Publishers gratefully acknowledges the support for its publishing
programs provided by the following agencies: the Government of Canada
through the Book Publishing Industry Development Program and the Canada
Council for the Arts, and the Province of British Columbia through the BC Arts
Council and the Book Publishing Tax Credit.

Cover design by Teresa Bubela
Cover illustration by Blair Drawson

Orca Book Publishers
PO Box 5626, Stn.B
Victoria, BC Canada
V8R 6S4

Orca Book Publishers
PO Box 468
Custer, WA   USA
98240-0468

www.orcabook.com
Printed and bound in Canada.

11 10 09 08 • 6 5 4 3 2

CHAPTER 1

My name is TJ Barnes, and I can't name the capital of Peru. I don't know what year the Wright brothers flew the first airplane. I can't instantly tell you how many dozen hot dogs you'll need if forty-two football players eat two each. When Mr. Phelps asked me to be on the school *Quiz Kids* team, I knew I had to straighten him out right away.

"You don't want me," I said. "You want Amanda Baker."

Amanda is so smart it's scary. She's also the nicest kid in our class, so you can't even hate her for being smart.

"Amanda is the team captain," said Mr. Phelps. "Please sit down, TJ."

I sat. I was trying to act cool, but my heart was thumping away as if I were a small frightened rodent. Being called to the vice-principal's office makes me feel guilty even if I haven't done anything wrong.

"You still really don't want me," I said. "You need super-smart kids. Try the other classes."

"Maria and Rashid are on the team already," said Mr. Phelps. "And although your brain power is perfectly solid, it's not your IQ I'm after."

IQ stands for intelligence quotient—that's something I do know. I've done the pop-up tests on the Internet. The tests show my IQ is—ta-da!—incredibly average.

"But isn't that what *Quiz Kids* is all about?" I asked. "The smartest kids in our school go against the smartest kids in Fairview school, and the brainiest team takes the prize."

"We've done that three years in a row, and we've lost three years in a row," said Mr. Phelps.

It was true. I'd seen it happen in our gym with the entire school, hundreds of parents, and reporters from the community newspaper watching. This year the local TV station was coming to broadcast *Quiz Kids* live on cable. I was pretty sure Fairview had invited them. Why would our school want everyone to watch us lose again?

Mr. Phelps straightened some papers on his desk.

"In school subjects, we've always done as well as the Fairview team. It's in the extra information area that we fall down. It will help that Maria, Rashid and Amanda all have different interests, but that still leaves us with the oddball questions."

The word "oddball" gave me a hint of where our talk was headed.

"Our team needs someone who knows quirky, out-of-the ordinary facts," said Mr. Phelps. "Someone who's done projects with unusual information about cats, for instance, or inventions or rockets or sports."

He still had the wrong person.

"You want Seymour," I said as I stood up. "I'll go get him for you."

Seymour is my best friend. He attracts strange facts the way the glowing lure on the head of an anglerfish attracts lunch. I only knew about anglerfish because Seymour told me. He even demonstrated by taping a flashlight to his head and wiggling his peanut butter sandwich closer and closer to the light until, *snap*, the sandwich was devoured.

Mr. Phelps, however, was waving me back to my chair.

"Wait, TJ. You worked on those projects with Seymour. And as much as I like Seymour, as much as I like his enthusiasm, his energy..."

Okay, it didn't take an IQ of a zillion to figure it out. Even I know that Seymour goes overboard in the excitement department. I could already picture the enthusiasm he'd bring to *Quiz Kids*, especially since the TV station was going to provide official podiums and answer buzzers. The moment he had an answer—any answer, including a wild guess—he'd be pushing the buzzer like crazy. He might even push the buzzers for the other team. Maybe he wasn't the best person for that kind of situation, but it would sure make things more interesting. *Quiz Kids* can get very, very boring when your team is losing.

"You're my choice, TJ," said Mr. Phelps. "Agreed?"

I didn't know what to say. Seymour was the one who came up with most of the amazing facts for our projects. How was he going to feel if I was on the team and he wasn't?

"Of course, Seymour can still work on research with you," said Mr. Phelps. "He could be your 'oddball fact' trainer. He could be trainer for the whole team."

It was when he added the last bit that I really understood. Mr. Phelps wanted Seymour's brain, but not his buzzer finger.

"You're only asking me so you can get Seymour's help without having to put up with him being on the team!" I said.

"I'm being practical, TJ," said Mr. Phelps. "This school can win. It deserves to win."

"I won't do it," I said. "Seymour's my best friend. He's the one who'd love being on *Quiz Kids*. Not me."

Mr. Phelps considered this for a moment.

"Please wait here," he said. He stood up and walked out the door.

Oh joy, now I was alone in the vice-principal's office. What if the phone rang—was I supposed to answer? What if a parent came in—would they think I'd been bullying some defenseless little kid?

Luckily, it wasn't long before Mr. Phelps returned with Seymour. As they came into the office, I heard Mr. Phelps talking about Amanda, Maria and Rashid, so I knew they'd already covered that part.

"Hey, TJ," said Seymour. "I thought you were in big trouble and you hadn't let me in on it! But Mr. Phelps says it's about *Quiz Kids*. Have you ever noticed the way our team always misses the easy stuff?"

Which pretty much proved Mr. Phelps's point. Seymour thinks of it as "easy stuff" because short, fast, amazing facts—the quirkier the better—are the kind that Seymour notices and remembers. He isn't so good with the actual dates dinosaurs lived, but he'll talk for half an hour about all sorts of bizarre things, like dinosaurs that had holes in their skulls and the ones that swallowed rocks.

"Okay, here's the deal," said Mr. Phelps, sitting down behind his desk. "There is one regular spot and one back-up spot on the *Quiz Kids* team. I would like the two of you to fill the spots and work together to cover the unusual information we might miss. A few days before the competition, I'll decide who will be on the team."

Talk about sneaky! Mr. Phelps and I both knew that he'd already decided, but since Seymour didn't know, he got sucked into the plan right before my very eyes.

"This is super!" said Seymour. "TJ and I are great at finding all sorts of neat facts. What kind do you want? Hair balls? Scabs? Hurricanes? Fortune-telling? Vomit?"

"I'm not going to tell you what to research," said Mr. Phelps. "All the questions that I think of fall into schoolwork categories. But the weird stuff...I don't even know where to start."

"You mean like what does a jellyfish have in common with cat pee?" asked Seymour.

"Definitely a question I wouldn't think of asking," said Mr. Phelps.

"And how many times do you have to pet a cat to generate enough energy to run a lightbulb?" asked Seymour.

"Has someone really figured that out?" asked Mr. Phelps.

"And if you suffer from doraphobia, what are you afraid of?" asked Seymour.

"Being squished between elevator doors," guessed Mr. Phelps.

"*Neeerk*," said Seymour, which is the sound he makes for a *no* buzzer. "We'll do it. Right, TJ?"

My mind was going a million miles a minute. I couldn't ruin things for Seymour, but I couldn't let Mr. Phelps get away with everything either.

"We should be allowed to decide for ourselves," I said. "When the time comes, Seymour and I should get to decide who goes on the team."

Mr. Phelps, however, was already shaking his head.

"No, I can't agree to that," he said. "But I'll tell you what. As of right now, the slate is clean. I'm going into this with an open mind. I promise to be fair. I mean that, TJ."

I thought of asking him to put it in writing and sign it, like the contracts Mom and Dad draw up for our business, but I didn't want to push my luck.

The PA system was crackling, which meant it was almost the end of the day. Seymour and I hurried back to class so we'd be ready to leave when the bell rang. When we hit the street, however, Seymour stopped at the corner to look back at the building.

"One of us is going to be a Quiz Kid for our school," he said. "Amazing!"

Seymour was even more excited than I'd expected. That reminded me of the questions he'd asked Mr. Phelps. I was pretty sure I knew some of the answers.

"Jellyfish and cat pee both glow under black light," I said.

"*Bing*," said Seymour, which is his *yes* sound.

"A doraphobic is someone who is afraid of fur," I said.

"*Bing*," said Seymour again.

"But I've got no idea how many times you have to pet a cat in order to turn on a lightbulb," I said.

"Some university student figured it out, but I forget the answer," said Seymour. "But that's okay—bluffing can be part of *Quiz Kids*. Cats are a good subject for us to bluff about. We'll have to remember that."

It was my Gran's four crazy cats that started us collecting amazing facts in the first place. These days I had two cats of my own. They were young and energetic and caused all kinds of trouble. We were still learning about cats.

Just then a white cube van pulled up beside us. The driver's hat was covered in paint spatters, his shirt collar was torn, he hadn't shaved for a day or two and his glasses were taped together over the bridge of his nose. Dad was definitely in the middle of a job.

"Hey, guys, do you have some time?" He had to shout because our truck goes *blup, blup, blup,* plus there seemed to be a new sort of howling noise in the back. "I've got some paint and flooring that I could use a hand unloading."

Seymour and I jumped in beside him. We like going out on jobs with Dad, and he usually treats us to a slushie after we finish helping him.

"Where to?" asked Seymour.

"Fairview Heights," said Dad, wheeling the truck around a corner toward the big hill above town.

"Perfect," said Seymour. "Time to check out the competition."

Dad was coaxing the truck into a lower gear so he didn't hear Seymour, which was good because I didn't feel like explaining *Quiz Kids* to my parents. And as for checking out the competition,

I figured that was just one of Seymour's crazy ideas.

If I ever tell you I can see into the future, don't believe a word I say.

CHAPTER 2

When my parents owned a hardware store, Seymour and I liked making wild guesses about our customers based on the kinds of tools, toys and gadgets they purchased. Now that my parents had switched to renovations and home decorating, the guessing game had taken on a different twist.

"Give us a hint," said Seymour. "Do they want the place painted Pickle?"

Pickle is a color on the paint charts. We hadn't seen anyone use it, but Seymour kept hoping.

"Nope," said Dad. "Oyster Bay, Malted Milk and Full Moon."

"Beachcomber," I guessed. The higher

up the hill we drove, the fancier the houses became. "Rich beachcomber."

"My guess is a world traveler who saves money by living on his favorite malted milk chocolate bars that he buys on sale at home," said Seymour. "And he's boring too. No zip in those colors. I think your mom should have thrown in some Gecko Green. Or Knockout Orange. Or...Pyromaniac."

"You made up the last one," I told Seymour.

"Do you think it would sell?" he asked.

"Might increase the cost of fire insurance...," said Dad. He stopped in mid-sentence to listen. "Do you hear that?"

"That howling noise?" I asked.

Dad nodded. "It started after I went down our back alley to pick up some things from the house. I've been hoping it's just dust in the brakes, but it should have worked its way out by now. The last thing we need is a big truck repair."

We were on top of the hill now. Thick hedges curtained both sides of the road.

Dad turned at a rock cairn marked with a brass number. At the end of the lane stood a huge house in a grove of trees all its own.

"Talk about cheap," said Seymour. "A house this size and they still travel with suitcases of chocolate bars from home!"

"That's because they own the chocolate bar factory," said Dad.

Sometimes it's hard to tell whether Dad is joking or telling the truth.

He cut the engine and the *blup, blup, blup* stopped but the howling didn't. Without the engine noise, it didn't sound as mechanical as it had before.

Seymour looked at me. One eyebrow went up, and one eyebrow went down.

"Sounds like the time T-Rex fell into the laundry hamper and couldn't get out," he said.

"Only louder," I added.

Dad laid his forehead against the steering wheel.

"Please tell me it's not," he said.

Seymour and I were already scrambling out the door.

"T-Rex?" called Seymour, pressing his face up against the side of the box. "Is that you?"

T-Rex is one of my cats. We'd named him after Seymour's favorite dinosaur.

Meoooooooow!

"You okay in there, buddy?" called Seymour.

Dad came around to the back of the van.

"Did you bring the laundry basket with the overalls in it?" I asked.

I'd seen the cats sleeping there that morning.

"I was in a hurry," said Dad, nodding. "I didn't turn on the light. I dropped the rags on top and headed out. I thought it was heavy, but I was carrying all kinds of stuff."

Dad worked the lever and rolled the door upward. The full force of T-Rex's misery came flowing out.

MEOOOOOOW!

T-Rex is long, lean and lanky. He has golden eyes, gray stripes and two white paws that look like those old-time shoe covers Gran says are called spats. He was sitting on the highest spot he could find, an old-fashioned desk that Mom had rescued and was hoping to sell, and he was howling his loudest. When he finally realized the door was open, he stopped howling and stared at us—two great round eyes in a furry striped face.

Seymour and I laughed.

"There's Alaska," I said.

Bits of black, orange and white fur showed through the holes of the basket. A pair of emerald green eyes squinted from the top. Alaska looked like she'd just woken up.

T-Rex took two steps toward us. Seymour climbed inside and scooped him up.

"No escaping," said Seymour. "But you can look out if you like."

"Good plan," said Dad. "Seymour, you cat-sit while TJ and I unload."

Seymour and T-Rex settled just inside the back door of the truck. Dad handed me two paint cans and took some of the flooring himself. As we started up the steps,

17

the front door opened and Mr. G. came out. He used to work for us at the store and now he helps Dad out on renovation jobs. He's also an awesome football coach. I like Mr. G. a lot.

"Hey, TJ!" he said.

"Seymour's here too, but he's got to look after the cats," I said.

Seymour waved one of T-Rex's paws from the back of the truck.

"Stowaways," said Dad.

Mr. G. laughed as I followed Dad through the front door. Yup, the place was huge. The entrance was about three times the size of our living room, with a wide staircase curving up to the landing above. It was also a mess. The floor had been torn up. There were piles of old wallpaper. Next to the stairs were drop sheets, a roller, a paint tray and a tin of paint with the lid resting lightly on top.

"Are they redoing the whole house?" I asked.

"Just the entrance and the den," said Mr. G., pointing to the wall he'd just begun to paint. "Malted Milk looks pretty much like its name."

It did too—smooth, creamy and just the right shade next to the wood of the stair rails. Mom's great at decorating. That's why our business is called Rooms by Rita.

It took us a few more trips to bring everything in. I was headed back to the truck to hang out with Seymour and the cats when Dad handed me a water bottle.

"TJ, slip off your shoes and see if you can find the kitchen and fill this up. It's too tall for the washroom sink."

I took the jug and headed around a corner. Then I stopped. Wow. I knew the house was big, but I didn't know it was gigantic.

The living room looked like something from a movie—a movie about *rich* people—with a high, high ceiling and white carpet that went on forever. To one side was a room that looked like an art gallery: paintings, small sculptures, expensive-looking books. In the middle of it was a sleek black grand piano with the top raised on a slant, like the wing of a bird. In the main room were oversize sofas and chairs and a sunken area with a gigantic stone fireplace. The far wall was all windows. There was a view of the town and the valley and the mountains far beyond. Everything was super-clean and super-shiny. Even in my socks I felt like tiptoeing. I'd got as far as the huge dining room when all of a sudden I heard barking. Lots of barking.

Woof, woof, woof, woof, woof.

Oh no—a dog! I raced back through the house. I could hear Seymour shouting from somewhere outside. "T-Rex, come back!"

I reached the front door just as a gray blur came shooting into the house and flying up the stairs.

"Look out!" cried Dad.

A second furry body, much larger than T-Rex, came hurtling by me, barking like crazy. Paint and wallpaper flew everywhere. I took the stairs two at a time after T-Rex; the dog was hot on his heels.

Up the stairs, around the corner.

SSSSSSSSSSSSSS.

High in a window alcove sat T-Rex, safely out of reach of the dog that was pawing the wall and barking. T-Rex was puffed up to about four times his regular size, and the noise he made was pure wild. He wasn't hiding from the dog, however. He was leaning over the edge and taking swipes at the dog's nose with his claws. I couldn't believe it. T-Rex was tough!

"If that cat hurts my dog you'll be very, very sorry."

I turned. A girl dressed in a school uniform was standing behind me. She was about my own age, with blond hair and blazing blue eyes.

"I mean it. Get him away from Froo Froo!"

A dog the size of an elephant was named Froo Froo? I was supposed to save a dog with gigantic teeth from one little cat? Then I remembered the mess downstairs. I didn't want to make a bad situation worse. I reached toward T-Rex.

SSSSSSSS.

T-Rex was in full defense mode. I turned back to the girl.

"He'll scratch me to pieces!" I said to her. "I'll be hamburger!"

The girl's eyes still blazed.

"Call off your dog," I said. "I'll get the cat calmed down and get him out of here."

The girl looked at the dog and me and the cat. She wasn't happy, but she turned her attention to the dog.

"Froo Froo, stop it. Sit. Sit."

Froo Froo didn't sit, but he switched from barking frantically to yelping and turning in circles. The girl grabbed him by the collar and heaved him to one side.

"Come," said the girl. "Come. I want to make sure you're okay."

The dog went with her down the hall. It even wagged its tail. Of course it couldn't resist a longing look over its shoulder toward T-Rex. The girl couldn't resist a last look either.

"You'd better get him out before Mom gets home," she called. "She'll have a fit if there's cat hair all over."

I waited until I heard a door shut firmly down the hall; then I went to the railing and looked over to see how much damage had been done. Seymour was standing just inside the front door.

"I'm sorry, Mr. Barnes. I'm really sorry."

"Did both cats escape?" asked Dad.

"Alaska's still in the truck," said Seymour. "I closed the door."

"Good," said Dad.

"But I couldn't hold T-Rex," said Seymour. "I'm sorry."

"It's all right, Seymour. We didn't know a dog was going to turn up," said Dad. He looked up and saw me at the railing. "How are things up there, TJ?"

"We're okay," I said. "He just needs a minute to calm down."

Seymour came charging up the stairs. Mr. G. followed him with a rag, wiping up kitty tracks the color of malted milk.

"Look how far he jumped," said Mr. G., pointing. "Paw prints here...and then way up here. Never saw a cat move so fast in my life."

Mr. G.'s shoulders began to quiver. And then to shake. I could tell he didn't want to laugh right out loud—when you're working in someone's house and things go wrong, you try to just keep it low-key and get everything back to normal as soon as you can—but the effort of keeping it inside brought tears to his eyes. He wiped them away with the cuff of his shirt.

"TJ, are there any more cat tracks higher up?" asked Dad.

The hallway and the nook where T-Rex had taken refuge were miraculously free of Malted Milk marks. Whew.

"All clear!" I called.

"Boy, look how puffy he is," said Seymour.

"He was twice that size before," I told him. "I think I can get him down now."

I reached for T-Rex. This time he didn't try to attack me. Mind you, he was still armed and dangerous. It was kind of like carrying a stiff-legged porcupine down the stairs. Mr. G.'s shoulders started to shake again.

"I'll finish up here," he said. "You'd better get the fur balls back home."

Dad waved us toward the door.

"All clear," said Seymour, making sure some other danger wasn't lurking outside. I didn't want to get this far only to be torn apart by T-Rex's claws and have him escape again.

"Can he ride in the front?" I asked.

"In the back," said Dad firmly. "It's safer for all of us."

Seymour made sure Alaska didn't slip out while Dad opened the back of the van just high enough for T-Rex to go shooting safely inside. We climbed into the cab, and Dad headed the van down the drive.

Just in time too. A long, low car—steel gray with blacked-out windows—passed us halfway down the lane. The dark windows gave it a definite air of foreboding. Seymour shifted in his seat so he could watch in the passenger side mirror as the car pulled up in front of the house.

"Mafia," said Seymour.

In the back of the van, the howling began once more.

CHAPTER 3

"Ask me what kind of silk is stronger than steel," said Seymour.

"Spider silk," answered Rashid.

"Ask me what entire continent doesn't even belong to anyone," said Seymour.

"Antarctica," said Maria.

"Ask me which has the largest number of neck bones—mice, humans or giraffes," said Seymour.

"They all have the same number," said Amanda.

"Rats," said Seymour. "I'm going to have to come up with better questions."

It was Wednesday after school. Seymour and I had gone to our first *Quiz Kids* meeting in the science room.

Maria was frowning hard at Seymour.

"The idea isn't to come up with questions," she said. "The idea is to come up with answers."

"Same thing," said Seymour.

"It's not the same at all," said Maria. "We aren't going to be able to choose our questions."

"But they *were* exactly the kind of oddball questions that get asked sometimes," said Amanda, trying to smooth things over. "Seymour knew the answers. So did we. That's good for the entire team."

Which was true, but Seymour had been wanting to arrive in a blaze of glory, an idea that had just been flushed down the toilet. Maria, meanwhile, was setting a stack of papers on the table.

"We need to focus," said Maria, picking up the top sheet. "Here's the schedule. Amanda, you did Greek myths this week, right?"

"Zeus and the gang on Mt. Olympus," said Amanda.

"Rashid, you did capital cities?"

"Beijing to Oslo," said Rashid. "And a few places in between."

"And I did…"

"What are you talking about?" asked Seymour. "What schedule?"

"Our *Quiz Kids* training schedule," said Maria. "Mr. Phelps laid it out for us. This is week eight and…"

"But this is the first meeting," said Seymour.

Maria looked at him as if he were crazy.

"*Quiz Kids* is only three weeks away. We wouldn't have a chance if we only started now," she said. "We've been working really hard for two months already."

"That's not fair," said Seymour. "TJ and I just started."

Maria turned abruptly to Amanda.

"You explain it to him," she said. "I'll go get the bells."

"Maria really wants to win," said Rashid as Maria headed out the door. "I mean she really, really wants to win."

"Why did Mr. Phelps wait until now to put Seymour and me on the team?" I asked.

"The fourth person was Winston, but he moved last week," said Amanda.

"Maria and Mr. Phelps had a big fight about who should replace him," said Rashid. "You weren't her first choice. Or her second. Or…"

"We get the picture," I said.

Rashid grinned.

"You'll be okay," he said. "We've got notes from all eight weeks for you. It's just a review of things we've learned in class anyway. It'll be fun to have two more people on the team."

I was beginning to like Rashid, but the file he handed us was huge.

"We didn't have an alternate before, so you'll have to share," said Amanda.

Sharing wouldn't be a problem. I couldn't read my way through the stack in a year, let alone a few weeks. Seymour was shaking his head.

"That isn't why Mr. Phelps put us on the team," he said. "TJ and I are supposed to do our own research. That's the whole point."

Just then Mr. Phelps himself came briskly through the door.

"Everyone ready for this week's quiz?" he asked.

"I've got the bells," said Maria, hot on his heels.

They were those silver "ring for service" bells that Mom places on the counter when she's in the back room at the store. Right away, Seymour hit his a few times. *Ding, ding, ding.* Everyone looked at him.

"Just making sure mine works," he said.

"All right," said Mr. Phelps. "Seymour and TJ, you've just joined the team, but feel free to ring in if you know the answers."

Ding. It was Seymour, just letting Mr. Phelps know he understood.

"We start with multiple choice. Anyone may buzz in and answer at any time. A frog is: a) a mammal, b) a reptile or c)—"

Amanda rang in and answered "amphibian" even before Mr. Phelps got to it.

"She can't do that!" protested Seymour.

"Yes, she can," said Maria. "Fairview did it all the time last year. It's one of the ways they beat us."

After that, Rashid and Maria rang in almost as fast.

"The imaginary line marking the separation between the northern and southern hemisphere is: a) the Tropic of Cancer, b) the arctic cir—"

Ding.

"The equator," answered Rashid.

"The process an insect undergoes when changing from larva to adult is called: a) photosynthesis, b) meta—

Ding.

"Metamorphosis," answered Maria.

"I knew that," Seymour said a couple of times, but he never hit the bell soon enough.

"Now we'll do a rapid round," said Mr. Phelps. "The capital of China is—"

Off they went again. Capital cities. Scientific definitions. Seymour and I didn't even get one of them. Finally he couldn't stand it anymore.

Ding. Ding. Ding. Ding. Ding.

Everyone stopped to look at him.

"True," he said.

"What's true?" asked Mr. Phelps.

"Lightning is five times hotter than the surface of the sun," said Seymour. "True."

"That wasn't the question," said Maria.

"But it could be the question," said Seymour. "If the subject was weather and if it was *true or false* time."

"But it wasn't," said Maria. "And it isn't."

"Are you sure you've got it right?" asked Amanda. "The sun is really, really hot."

"I'm sure," said Seymour. "That's what makes it a good question. That's why they might ask it. It's tricky. It's neat. It's amazing."

Maria scowled. Mr. Phelps looked thoughtful. He turned in my direction.

"TJ," he said. "Any thoughts?"

Why was he asking me? Just because I thought Seymour should be on the team didn't mean I could control him. Besides, I like Seymour the way he is.

"It's hard to practice oddball answers if there aren't any oddball questions," I said.

Mr. Phelps nodded.

"Seymour," he said, "try to keep it under control."

After that, Seymour rang the bell after every third question and provided us with an oddball fact.

"For every human on earth there are two hundred million insects."

"Raindrops are shaped like hamburger buns."

Maria began sending him dirty looks.

"Fish scales make lipstick shine."

"Seventy-five percent of the dust in your house is dead skin cells."

Maria's glare became more intense.

"Grasshoppers have ears on their knees."

"Your brain can remember five hundred times the number of facts in a set of encyclopedias."

If Maria had had an encyclopedia, I think she would have hit him with it. Luckily, at that point, Seymour ran out of amazing facts. He seemed to think he'd made a good start, however, and sat there happily, his finger on the bell just in case. As for me, I didn't answer anything or come up with any amazing facts. I just sat there like a lump. And my head was hurting from all the *dings*.

Amanda walked partway home with us.

"Are you sure there are two hundred million insects for *every* person on earth?" she asked.

"That's what the bug books say," replied Seymour.

"Amazing," said Amanda.

"Exactly," said Seymour.

"What amazes me is how hard Maria tries," I said. "She gets totally upset when she doesn't have the right answer."

"I know," sighed Amanda. "It's good, I guess. I mean, it will help us win. Fairview's a really competitive school. Lots of the parents are bankers and lawyers and…"

"And people who own chocolate bar factories," said Seymour.

At least he didn't say Mafia. Even I knew my parents weren't working for the mob.

"So what? We've got kids whose parents are lawyers too," I said.

"Fairview has more of them," said Amanda. "And they put a lot of money into extra programs for the school."

"So you're saying we don't have a hope of winning?" I asked.

"I'm just saying that it's not exactly bad that Maria is trying so hard," said Amanda. "She goes a little overboard, but we all have to work really hard or we're going to lose as miserably as last year."

"I can see that I need a lot more facts," said Seymour.

"And I need to get started on what Mr. Phelps has assigned for next week," said Amanda.

They headed off in opposite directions. I should have just drifted along thinking about other things.

But I didn't. I hadn't liked not knowing any of the answers. I hadn't liked sitting there like a lump.

I thought about *Quiz Kids* all the way home.

CHAPTER 4

"TJ? Ten minutes and counting."

Saturday mornings, Dad and I have breakfast at the kind of fast-food place Mom says isn't good for us. Even so, I usually sleep until the last possible minute. This time I jumped up as soon as Dad called. I wanted time to check that the cats were safely in the house before we headed out. No more surprises, please.

Alaska was easy to find. She was buried deep in the clothes on my bedroom floor, sound asleep. I was supposed to pick up the clothes, but how could I disturb her beauty rest?

Finding T-Rex took longer. I looked in his usual spots. He wasn't on top of the hot-air vents. He wasn't behind the sofa. He wasn't lying flat on a chair under the dining room table. Then I spotted the old desk. Dad had brought it in from the truck until Mom could find someone to buy it. I remembered that it had cubby-holes all along the top. Hmmm. I walked around to the front of the desk. Yup— there was T-Rex. He'd crammed himself into the longest of the cubbyholes. He looked totally happy. Squished but happy. Hey—maybe I could turn the desk into a cat condo, a fancy house for cats!

"Where to?" I asked, licking the ketchup from my fingers about an hour later.

"First stop is your gran's," said Dad. "We're going to give her a new kitchen floor while she's trekking through the rain forest. I need to do some measuring before she leaves."

My gran doesn't have enough money to go on many trips, not even if she takes her own chocolate bars, so when she does travel she makes the most of it. When she went to Hawaii she spent her time climbing volcanoes, not sitting on the beach. Mind you, even at home, Gran is pretty interesting. For instance, some older people have doilies and cushions decorating the living room. My gran has cats—four of them.

An orange cat with a bent tail was spread across the sofa.

"Hi, Kink," I said, stroking him from head to tail.

A fluffy calico cat was draped over the easy chair. She's the mother of my own two cats.

"Hi, Cleo," I said. "The kids are fine." I was careful not to ruffle her fur because Cleo thinks she's the most beautiful cat in the world, and she doesn't like to be mussed up.

A black cat was peering around the curtains. She's a scaredy-cat, so Gran gave her a special name to help her gain confidence.

"Hi, Killer," I said. I patted her exactly twice. One pat too many and Killer streaks off for quieter places.

A fourth cat was lying on something colorful that was spread across the dining room table. Maximilian the Emperor is large and white with gleaming blue eyes. He was lying on a map of the world. He covered most of it. I didn't say hi to him— over half of all white cats with blue eyes are deaf, and Max is one of them—but I did scratch him under the chin.

"Are you sure you don't want me to look after them while you're gone?" I asked.

"Not this time, thank you, TJ," said Gran. "A friend is coming in."

"Where exactly is Belize?" I asked, trying to see around Max. "Is it really rain forest?"

"Max, kindly move your butt so I can show TJ where I'm going," said Gran.

Cats never do what you tell them to do, even if they can hear. It was only when Gran began to pull the map out from beneath him that he rolled over as if he'd meant to do it all along.

"Central America," said Gran, pointing. "And yes, there are rain forests. I still can't quite believe I'm going. My friend Gladys is paying my airfare. Her sister's been helping set up a school in a small village, and Gladys wants to visit, but she's afraid to travel alone."

"Forty-five-year-old Gladys is nervous, so she's taking along your seventy-two-year-old grandmother," said Dad, smiling.

It sounded weird but we both knew Gran, so it made perfect sense.

"TJ, I'd like to borrow that great big suitcase, the one your mom packed all your clothes and stuffed animals and toys into when you were little and used to come for a visit," said Gran. "Do you still have it?"

"I think so," I said. "But I thought you used a backpack."

"I do. The suitcase is for the clothing and school supplies for the kids at the new school. We have a list of what they need so we can be sure to bring the right things. We'll see the rain forest and then we'll help out at the school."

I was right. No beach-sitting for Gran.

"But I'm really sorry that I'll miss you and Seymour on *Quiz Kids*," said Gran.

Dad looked up from rummaging for a tape measure in his toolbox.

"TJ, are you on the *Quiz Kids* team?" he asked. "Why didn't you tell us?"

"I guess I forgot," I said. It's easy to forget something you don't want to think about. "How did you find out, Gran?"

"I saw the list of team members on the local cable announcements," said Gran. "I think your vice-principal has a relative at the station."

So much for my idea about the other school being behind the TV broadcast. And I didn't know they were going to advertise ahead of time! Maybe I should have read the permission slip before I forged my mom's signature.

"That's neat, TJ," said Dad.

"Are you excited?" asked Gran.

"I'm just the backup," I said. "Seymour's the one who's really going to be on the team."

Gran looked at me in a funny sort of way. Before she could say anything, however, there was a mad skittering sound in the kitchen. Kink was chasing Dad's measuring tape.

"We'll figure this by the square foot because that's the way the tiles come," said Dad. "The kitchen is ten feet square. The tiles are ten dollars a square foot."

"One hundred dollars," I said. "That's got to be good."

"Not quite," said Dad. "Ten feet square means ten feet long and ten feet wide, like a giant chessboard but with two extra rows."

Right away I knew my mistake.

"You'll need one hundred squares," I said. "That's a lot more. That's a thousand dollars."

"But installation is free," said Dad.

"Which is why I can afford it and still be a world traveler. Amazing!" said Gran. "Run the idea of a chessboard pattern by your mom, TJ. I'm letting her decide on the final design."

"I'll ask her about the suitcase too," I called as we left.

At the next stop, Dad had curtain rods to install, a job I could help him with even if all I did was hold things in place. Then it was time to go meet Mom at the shop.

"Looks like the Jessops are here," said Dad, pulling into one of our parking spots at the back.

At first I didn't know who the Jessops were, and then I spotted the Mafia car. A moment later I spotted the girl with the blue eyes. She was sitting on some steps just down from our back entrance, wearing jeans and a T-shirt and looking totally bored. Beside her was Froo Froo, panting away happily with a goofy dog-grin on his face.

"You can bring him inside if you like," called Dad as he climbed out of the truck.

"I'd better not," sighed the girl. "He's in Mom's bad books. He ate her new shoes this morning."

Dad nodded and headed into the back of the store. I was about to follow, but the girl pointed toward the open window of the truck.

"Is your deranged cat in there?"

I turned back.

"He's not deranged! He was afraid, that's all. And we don't usually travel with a cat. It was an accident."

"Oh," said the girl. I should have gone inside then, but something about that "oh" bugged me.

"And in case you haven't noticed, your dog isn't exactly small and helpless," I added.

"He's big, but he's still a puppy," said the girl, putting an arm around him. "He can get in trouble really fast."

"A puppy? He's monster-size!"

"He grew a little bigger than he was supposed to, but it's not his fault!" the girl said. "I keep telling M—"

"Is that why you gave him a goofy name like Froo Froo? Because you thought he'd be small?" I asked.

"It's not goofy; it's entirely appropriate," said the girl. "It's short for Fruitful Foresters' Fancy the Third. His parents are both pedigreed. He's even entered in the dog show next month. I won't actually take him in the ring, of course. The trainer does that."

Deranged, entirely appropriate, pedigreed—it was almost like she spoke a different language. I guess it went with the Mafia car, the huge house and the dog trainer.

"Maybe the dog trainer could teach him not to chase cats," I said.

"Maybe you could train your cat not to be vicious," said the girl.

"T-Rex isn't vicious!" I insisted.

As soon as the words were out of my mouth, I realized what I'd done. Oh no.

"T-Rex?" asked the girl, her eyes growing wide. "You're making fun of me because I shorten my dog's name to Froo Froo, but you actually named your cat T-Rex?"

Just then the back door opened, and a woman in a red suit stepped out. Saved!

"Hi, Mom," I said. "You look great."

Mom dresses up at the shop because it's more professional for the new business. Dad and I have a pact to tell her how nice she looks to build up her self-confidence, kind of like what Gran does with Killer. Mom sees right through us, but she plays along.

"Thanks, TJ," she said. She turned to the girl with the dog. "Elizabeth, your mother has gone to the drugstore. She won't be long. I've brought water for Frooie."

"Thank you," said Elizabeth.

The phone in the shop began to ring. Mom handed me the container and went back inside. Elizabeth looked at me in a puzzled sort of way.

"Rita's your mom?" she asked.

I nodded as I set down the water. Frooie—anything was better than Froo Froo—went for it immediately. Big dog, big mouth, big tongue. *Glop, glop, glop.* I remembered one of Seymour's amazing facts...well not exactly amazing, but definitely interesting. I crouched down to get a better look.

"Rooms by Rita—it's a nice store, and some of your mom's ideas are extremely creative," said Elizabeth. "My mom doesn't hire anyone unless they're highly recommended."

Highly recommended? Extremely creative? Yup, we spoke a different language.

"I guess you go out in that old truck with the workman to check up on jobs and repor..." Elizabeth stopped in mid-sentence. "What are you doing?"

"The animal books are right—dogs drink backward," I said. "Cats lap forward, plus they have bumpy things on their tongues that help hold the water, but dogs bend their tongues backward. They kind of drop water wildly onto the bottom of their mouths."

Frooie had stopped just long enough for me to explain the facts to Elizabeth. Now he put his head down again. *Glop glop glop.*

"Like that," I said as water went sloshing everywhere.

"You're nuts," said Elizabeth.

"It's true!" I said.

"It might be true, but the back alley is a disgusting place to crawl around in," said Elizabeth.

Now that she mentioned it, I was practically eye-to-eye with the greasy napkins and squished French fries from the restaurant garbage down the alley. It smelled too. Gross.

"I better go inside," I said.

"Thank your mom again for the water," said Elizabeth.

The store was cool and welcoming. Mom had just hung up the phone.

"Everything all right, TJ?" she asked.

"Sure. Great," I answered. "Gran thinks her kitchen floor should be done in red and black squares so the cats can play chess on it. And she'd like to borrow our big suitcase."

"I didn't mean with Gran," said Mom. "I meant with Elizabeth."

I shrugged in my best casual manner.

"Oh that. Sure," I said. "She says thanks for the water. We were just talking about cats and dogs and stuff."

"Good," said Mom. "The Jessop job is important. Well, I'd better take over from your dad. He doesn't like to be out front in his work clothes."

Work clothes. Workman. My brain began to search backward. It didn't like what it came up with. Trust a girl who lived in a big fancy house to think every-one's dad dressed in a business suit and drove a shiny new car!

I opened the back door. Elizabeth's mother and Frooie were already in the car, and Elizabeth was just climbing in herself.

"He's my dad! He owns the business too! I travel with him because I like traveling with him!" I called. "And Mr. G. doesn't need anyone to check up on him!"

I don't know if she heard. The door on the Mafia car closed with an expensive *shwunk,* the motor purred to life and they were gone.

CHAPTER 5

"Splash!" said Seymour.

He was standing on the back of the sofa in our living room. He'd just opened his hands to release an invisible object, and now he was pointing down at the carpet.

"I just dropped a cannonball into the Mariana Trench, the deepest part of the Pacific Ocean," he explained. "Now we'll see how long it takes to reach the bottom."

He climbed down and settled on the cushions. When Seymour starts acting weird, it's best just to ignore him.

It was Sunday afternoon and we were hanging out at my house. I'd surrounded myself with *Quiz Kids* notes and I was trying to memorize the oceans in order of their size: Pacific, Atlantic, Indian, Southern, Arctic. I wanted to be able to answer at least a few of the questions next time we had a practice!

Seymour, on the other hand, was surrounded by books he'd found at the library. He couldn't help sharing what he discovered.

"Listen to this," he said. "People lose taste buds as they get older. No wonder adults like broccoli."

I was still trying to memorize: Pacific, Atlantic...

"This is neat," said Seymour. "House-flies can change direction four times in a single second."

Pacific, Atlantic, Southern, Indian...or was it Indian, Southern?

"Hurricane speed!" said Seymour. "That's how fast the wind from a sneeze can travel. Hurricane speed!"

I gave up on oceans and switched to continents: Asia, Africa...

"Geckos can't blink, so they wipe their eyes with their tongues," said Seymour.

"Wow. I can't even touch my nose with my tongue."

I didn't have to look at him to know that he was trying. Maybe I'd try planets instead. Jupiter, Saturn...

"I didn't know this!" said Seymour. "The Eiffel Tower is taller in hot weather."

At least that fact related to something in the file folders—metal expands when heated. The Eiffel tower is made of iron, and iron is a metal. I flipped to the stack of science notes. The scientific symbol for iron is *Fe* and that brought me to the entire periodic table, which we hadn't even studied. Now my head hurt.

"How can anyone remember all this stuff?" I asked.

"I've got a book about that too," said Seymour, shuffling through his pile. He brought out a book with a giant brain and the words *YOUR AMAZING MEMORY* on the cover. As soon as he opened the book, he found things to be amazed about. "Guess why telephone numbers are seven digits."

"No idea," I said.

"Because that's how many things a person can remember at a time—between five and nine. Most people max out at seven."

"That's not right," I said. "Even I can remember more than seven things. And you were talking the other day about brains holding more than umpteen encyclopedias…"

"That was long-term memory. Five to nine items is short-term memory; the book says to try it with a shopping list. I'll make one up. Apples, oranges, grapes, carrots, lettuce, celery…"

I began to repeat after Seymour, but almost immediately he frowned and shook his head.

"Hang on. Even I can't remember. I'll use one of the tricks from the book—association."

He looked at the cats.

"Alaska, your head is an apple," he said. "T-Rex, your head is an orange. The coffee table is covered in grape vines," he continued. "There's a giant carrot growing out the top. An even more giant rabbit is trying to pull it out but he's having trouble because he's rolling around on a huge lettuce. The rabbit has ears like celery sticks."

I got the idea—make up a wild story and fix it in place with objects around the room. I wasn't sure how it was going to help me with oceans.

"Oops!" said Seymour. "It's been ten minutes. I'd better check on the cannonball."

He jumped on the sofa with such an explosion of energy that apples and oranges—or rather cats—flew off in different directions. Once more, Seymour pretended to be in the middle of the ocean. He leaned out over the armrest, also known as the ship's rail, shaded his eyes against the glare of the water and peered down, down into the Mariana Trench.

"It hasn't hit the bottom yet," he said.

"Are you sure?" I asked. "Ten minutes is a long time to be falling, even if it is through water."

"Not even close," said Seymour. He sat on the carpet and picked up the memory book.

"There are competitions for memory. Some people can memorize forty or fifty entire decks of playing cards, all in order."

"I can't even remember the oceans in order of size!" I said.

"Pete Attwater Ignores Sneaky Aardvarks," said Seymour. He set down the memory book and picked up one with a giant insect on the cover. "Did you know some soldier ants explode to defend their colonies?"

I was still thinking about oceans. "Pete" was Pacific, "Attwater" was Atlantic. That was easy to remember. Pete owned the corner grocery store—Attwater's Emporium.

"Oh wow! It takes eighty thousand bees gathering nectar while flying the equivalent of three times around the world to make one jar of honey!" read Seymour.

"Ignores" was Indian. "Sneaky" was Southern. "Aardvarks" was Arctic. Pacific, Atlantic, Indian, Southern, Arctic. Yes!

"Chameleons can move their eyes in two different directions at the same time," said Seymour. He stretched his arms sideways and tried to see both of his hands at once.

"Have you got one for the continents?" I asked.

"Nope," said Seymour. "Make up your own. But planet is the Greek word for wanderer."

"How did you know I was trying to memorize planets too?"

Seymour just looked at me. Of course. They were standard questions. Everyone would be memorizing them.

"The cannonball should be on the bottom now," I said.

Seymour jumped up on the sofa again and once more shaded his eyes. "Nope," he said. "It's still..."

He froze in mid-sentence.

"What?" I asked.

"Shhhh!" said Seymour. He dropped down with his ear right against the carpet. He crawled to the wood floor of the dining room, listening all the way. He'd left the ocean book open, and I saw a quick fact.

"The longest anyone has ever stayed underwater without breathing is nine minutes," I said. "Tell me when you need rescuing."

"No...there's really something down there."

"In the basement?" I asked.

"In the floor," said Seymour.

"No, there isn't," I said.

"Yup, there is. Listen," said Seymour.

I couldn't help it. I knew I was probably getting sucked in, but I lay on my stomach with my ear to the floor anyway. Seymour was right. It was a very faint sound, but it was definitely something.

"How could there be something in the floor?" asked Seymour.

I'd been on enough renovation projects with Dad and Mr. G. to know the answer to that one. "Floor joists," I said. "Boards are put together in triangles and V-shapes to make the floor strong. There's space in between the floor of the living room and the ceiling of the basement."

"Maybe it's full of...exploding ants!" said Seymour.

I looked around the room.

"I wonder where the cats are," I said.

We found Alaska asleep among the clean towels in the closet—burrowing into warm soft places is a big attraction for Alaska—but we couldn't find T-Rex.

"Secret weapon time," said Seymour.

The best way to find a cat is to open a tin of salmon. As soon as I set the can on the counter I felt Alaska brushing my legs. Of course, if T-Rex was really in the floor joists, he might have missed the delicate *clink* of the can on the counter. I pierced the tin with the opener and began to turn the knob. Seymour was lying on the dining room floor, listening.

"He's on the move," said Seymour. "This way. No, this way. No! Back toward the front door."

We rounded the corner just in time to see T-Rex push his head through a spot where the baseboard had come loose and there was a crack between a beam and the floor. His body seemed to grow long and snaky as he pulled himself through.

"Proving once and for all that the shoulder blades on cats aren't attached the same way they are on humans," said Seymour.

"I don't think Dad would be keen on tearing up the floor to rescue T-Rex if he ever got stuck down there," I said.

Seymour and I blocked off the gap. After that we opened the tin of salmon and treated the cats while we tried to remember the shopping list from earlier. I did pretty well except I included the giant rabbit, which wasn't actually on the list. We made sandwiches for ourselves and decided to eat them in front of the TV. It was set to the cable channel that shows what's on TV, lists community events and shows the current time, second by second.

"I guess we missed the cannonball," I said.

"Nope, just about right," said Seymour. He jumped on the sofa. "Five, four, three, two, one—bingo!"

"It's been over an hour!" I said.

"That's how long it would take a cannonball to reach the deepest part of the ocean—an hour," said Seymour. "It's a very, very long way down."

My attention, however, had been pulled away by the TV. The blurb for *Quiz Kids* was rolling across the screen. There were our names, starting with *Amanda Baker* and ending with *TJ Barnes*.

That was the good part—seeing my name on TV. Next came the bad part.

"Oh no!" I said. "It's her!"

"Who?" said Seymour, sitting bolt upright on the living room floor, his head swiveling around like crazy. "Where?"

"The girl with the dog that tried to eat T-Rex. That's her name!"

I pointed at the TV. Second on the list for Fairview was *Elizabeth Ann Jessop*.

CHAPTER 6

The thing that really drives me crazy about life is how things snowball.

"I found out something strange," said Gran when she came to our place for supper the next night. "Gladys and I know someone else who's traveling to Belize—not when we leave here on the local flight but when we change to a larger plane at the international airport. My neighbor has a niece whose best friend's father is on the same flight to Belize as we are."

"It amazes me how often those kinds of coincidences happen," said Mom.

"Maybe not quite a coincidence," said Dad. "There's a theory called Six Degrees of Separation. The idea is that everybody on the planet has some sort of connection to everybody else through just six stages. If you do the math, it almost makes sense. Let's say I know one hundred people, and they each know one hundred people, and *they* each know one hundred people, all the way along through six levels. How many people is that, TJ?"

"Something with twelve zeros," I said. "A trillion?"

"I think so," said Dad. "Mind you, there are over six trillion people on the planet. And some people live in isolated communities where there wouldn't be as many connections with the outside world, so it might not work in all cases."

"But in North America it would make sense," said Gran. "Maybe it's not so strange that I'd know someone on the same plane...well, sort of know them."

And maybe it wasn't so strange that there would be a connection between our *Quiz Kids* team and the Fairview team. But why did it have to be Elizabeth with the *glop glop* dog? And why did I have to be the missing link?

Seymour had also been thinking about the connection.

"You know the girl with the dog, Elizabeth what's-her-name on the Fairview team?" he asked on the way to school the next morning. "You need to make friends with her. It's like I said—you can check out the competition."

"No, I can't," I told him.

"Sure you can," said Seymour. "Ask her about *Quiz Kids* without making it obvious. All those big houses have satellite TV, not cable. Even if she happens to know your name, she won't know that you're on the team. Find out how they study. Figure out their strategy."

"No," I said. "I'm not going anywhere near her."

"Why not?" asked Seymour.

"Because I'm pretty sure she thinks I'm an idiot," I said.

"Even better," said Seymour. "She won't suspect you!"

"She's not going to suspect me because

I'm not going to ask," I said. "And Dad's done at the Jessop house."

But when I dropped by the store after picking up a slushie, I discovered that things had changed. Dad had just come down from Fairview. Boy, was he steamed.

"Remember those two fellows we hired because they claimed to be the world's greatest flooring experts? They put in the wrong subfloor at the Jessop house. I caught them tiling over it to hide their 'mistake,' and you should have seen the mess they were making of that!"

Mom frowned. Dad kept ranting.

"'Just let it slide!' they told me. 'We'll cut you in. We'll all make a little extra money...your clients have lots of it. They won't even know.'"

"Oh dear," said Mom.

"Boy, I hate it when someone tries to cheat on a contract," said Dad. "I treat people fairly and I expect others to do the same. I sent them packing."

"You did the right thing," said Mom. "But now I don't know what we'll do.

The Jessops are away. I promised them that all the tiling would be done by the time they get back on Friday night."

"It won't be done by Friday," said Dad. "I can rip out the crappy stuff tonight and lay the proper subfloor myself between other jobs on Thursday. But I don't have enough experience with tile. I asked Tony, but he can't do it until Saturday. Plus you know what he charges on weekends. There goes whatever profit we hoped to make on the project."

Mom, however, was nodding in agreement.

"Tony will do a great job, and that would really help," she said. "The Jessop renovation is important. It could pull in all kinds of new clients for us up in Fairview. She's a professor at the university. He's a lawyer. They do a lot of entertaining—we couldn't get better advertising."

A university professor and a lawyer—I almost choked on my slushie. Elizabeth probably had an IQ of a zillion! And unless I thought of some way to duck out of it, I'd probably see her again this weekend.

One look at Dad, however, and I knew I wasn't going to try to duck out of anything. His hair was caked with drywall dust, and his glasses were taped together in two spots instead of one. He'd been working extra hard lately because Mr. G. was sick. He'd need my help on Saturday. I figured he could use a hand tonight too.

"If you're going back there tonight, I'll help you," I said.

"Not on a weeknight, TJ," said Dad, shaking his head.

"It's a weeknight for you too," I said. "It's not fair that you have to work all day and all night and lose money on top of everything."

"We'll both help," said Mom. "It won't take as long with all three of us."

Even then, it was late when we finished up at the Jessops' house. Dad was a whole lot happier about the situation, but maybe I was more tired than I realized. By the time *Quiz Kids* practice rolled around the next afternoon, I wasn't in a very good mood.

Seymour, on the other hand, was pumped. He arrived with a whole new set of amazing facts.

Ding.

"Hippos' sweat is red and acts as a sunblock."

Ding.

"The largest living thing is a fungus."

Maria was looking more and more like a storm cloud. Even Amanda and Rashid were having trouble concentrating. It wasn't just that Seymour was throwing in facts everywhere. It was that his *dings* were breaking the rhythm of question and answer. The others had been working hard studying their own material; it wasn't fair that Seymour kept ringing in wildly.

Ding.

"The fear of being naked is gymnotophobia."

Ding.

"The noises your stomach makes are called borborygmi."

Meanwhile, I was hoping to answer at least one question. Ask about oceans, I thought. Ask about oceans, ask about oceans.

"We now move to geography," said Mr. Phelps. "Name the third-largest ocean."

My brain blocked all distractions and zeroed in: Pete Attwater Ignores... Seymour must have been doing the same thing because—*Ding*—we both hit our bells at the same time.

"Indian," we said together.

Maria threw her hands in the air. She wasn't cheering.

"Didn't you hear? Amanda just answered that!" said Maria.

I turned to Amanda. She looked apologetic, but she nodded just the same. I guess I'd gone too far in the concentration department. I hadn't heard the bell or her answer. Brother. Meanwhile, Maria was ranting at Seymour.

"Don't you even listen? You have to keep up. You have to focus," said Maria.

"How can I focus when you're so busy being a bell hog?" countered Seymour.

"I'm not a bell hog!" said Maria.

"You ring in all the time!" said Seymour.

"I only ring in when I have the right answer to the right question at the right time!" said Maria. "And you are a complete and utter..."

Mr. Phelps interrupted in his calmest vice-principal manner. "Maria, I understand your frustration, but please don't overreact. This is a practice session, and *Quiz Kids* is not a matter of life and death. And Seymour, maybe you could..."

"TJ rang in too," said Seymour. "Why is it always me she complains about?"

"Because you're the one that constantly rings in to answer your own questions!" said Maria.

"Which is better than TJ, who never knows answers or questions or *anything!*" said Seymour.

That did it. Now he'd even made me mad.

"I know lots of things!" I said. "I just don't go blabbing them all over and driving everyone crazy!"

My voice had come out really, really loud. Everyone looked shocked, especially Seymour. He looked from Maria to Mr. Phelps to Amanda to Rashid. No one said a word. Finally he looked back at me. I didn't trust myself to say anything.

Seymour folded his arms, pressed his lips tightly together and stared off pointedly at nothing at all. The message was pretty clear. Not a single word was going to escape from his mouth, even if the roof was about to fall on us. It was Amanda who finally broke the silence.

"I think we're ready for more questions," she said.

Mr. Phelps went back to asking questions. Rashid, Maria and Amanda went back to coming up with answers. Seymour kept staring into space. Bit by bit, I forgot about him. I began concentrating on the questions. I'd been studying while Seymour had been dropping cannonballs. I answered a question about planets at the same time as Rashid—I forgot to ring in, so it wouldn't have counted in a game, but at least I answered it.

I answered the individual questions Mr. Phelps gave each of us. And then there was a math question. Dad does lots of math in his head when he figures things on the job, and he always includes me. It's like a game we play together. And this question was related to something we'd been talking about at Gran's just a few days ago.

"How many black squares are there on a chessboard?" asked Mr. Phelps.

Ding.

"Thirty-two," I answered.

"Correct," said Mr. Phelps.

When it was all over, Seymour headed out the door without me.

CHAPTER 7

As soon as I came through our gate that afternoon, I looked toward the front windows of our house. Alaska's green eyes were already peering through the glass. No matter what time of day I come home, her special cat-senses alert her and she comes to the window to watch for me. Today it felt especially good to see her friendly face.

I expected T-Rex to come running as soon as I opened the door. Instead I heard him howling.

Meow. Meow. Meow.

"T-Rex?" I called.

Meow, meow, meow.

Wherever he was, he wasn't happy.

Oh, brother. Here we go again, I thought.

I checked the vents, the spot behind the sofa and the dining room chairs. No T-Rex. I made sure the baseboard gap was still blocked off, and I lay on the floor and listened, just in case. Nope. The howling wasn't coming from the floor joists. I checked the laundry hamper. I checked the garbage. I even checked the downstairs toilet. No T-Rex.

I thought about opening a tin of salmon, but it was feeding time anyway. That's probably why he was howling so loudly.

Meow, meow, meow.

The trouble was he didn't keep howling. As soon as he heard me moving, he stopped. I guess he figured if I was on my way to the rescue, he didn't need to call for help anymore. I *was* coming to his rescue, but without the howling I couldn't find him!

I headed up to search the bedrooms. At the top of the stairs I heard him again, but the sound didn't seem to be coming from the bedrooms. It seemed to be coming from *outside* the bedrooms, through the screen of Mom and Dad's window at the side of the house.

Meow, meow, meow.

Oh no! He must have escaped when Dad came home for lunch!

I raced downstairs, out the front door and around the side of the house.

"T-Rex? T-Rex!" I called.

He wasn't anywhere in sight. I walked all around the house. I couldn't see him, but I could hear him again.

Meow, meow, meow.

Now it definitely sounded like he was *inside,* at the back of the house where the kitchen is. In fact I was sure of it. I knew the kitchen door would still be locked, so I raced around through the front again.

Meow, meow, meow.

I hurried through the house, but as soon as I hit the kitchen, of course the howling stopped. No cat to be seen.

I looked in the cupboards. I had a horrible thought and looked in the fridge and then the freezer and then—most horrible thought of all, except it wasn't turned on so I knew he was okay—I looked in the oven. No T-Rex.

I stood very, very, very still. I waited. And waited. And waited.

MEOW MEOW MEOW.

Good grief. The kitchen door was howling. Between the wooden kitchen door and the outside metal door there is a tiny, tiny space, barely the width of a few fingers. Sometimes, if the wooden door is open a bit, T-Rex goes into the space to snoop around. He couldn't possibly...

I opened the inside door. Out shot T-Rex. It was true. He'd been stuck in the tiny, tiny space between the doors. Dad must have shut the door without realizing he was there.

"T-Rex! Are you all right?"

Prrrrrrrrrrrr.

I had to tell someone. I phoned Gran. Gran is perfect for cat stories. I also remembered that I had a message to pass along from Mom.

"Guess what," I said when Gran picked up the phone. "T-Rex is the world's skinniest cat."

She laughed as I told her the entire story.

"How's the gang over there?" I asked.

"It's still ten days until my trip, and they already know I'm leaving," said Gran. "Last night Killer climbed inside my backpack. I think she wants to come with me to Belize."

"I want to come too, Gran," I said.

I didn't know how much I meant it until something in my own voice gave me away. There was a little moment of silence on the end of the phone, and then Gran asked, "What's wrong, TJ?" And when I didn't answer, she spoke again. "Does this have something to do with *Quiz Kids*? It's the same day that I leave, isn't it? How did practice go today?"

"I didn't mean to get mad at Seymour, Gran. And I didn't try to show him up on purpose," I said. "It's just that I knew some of the answers, and they just came flying out."

"My goodness," said Gran. "Are you admitting to a competitive streak, TJ? That's actually not surprising news.

Remember the science fair and the rockets? Remember football?"

"But I didn't mean to compete against Seymour," I said. "He's my friend. And he's really mad."

Even over the phone, I could hear Gran sigh.

"It's hard when friends are involved," she said. "But you and Seymour have known each other for a long time, TJ. You'll work it out."

Just as she said it, the doorbell sounded—two quick rings, the way Seymour always announces himself.

"That sounds like him now," said Gran. "I'll let you go."

"Wait!" I said.

"You need to talk to him, TJ," said Gran. "It's better to straighten things out right away."

"It's something else," I explained quickly. "Mom found the big suitcase. She has some school supplies left over from the hardware store, and she's looking for some clothing to send to Belize too."

"Excellent," said Gran. "Thanks, TJ. Bye."

Usually Seymour just double-rings and walks right in. When the rings came a second time, I realized I'd actually have to answer the door. I had no idea what I was going to say, but I opened it anyway.

Seymour was standing on the front step. He was frowning hard, one eyebrow up and one eyebrow down. That's what Seymour does when he's trying to work something out in his head.

"Your plan isn't working," he said.

"What plan?" I asked.

"Your plan to get me on the team," said Seymour. "You're the one Mr. Phelps really wanted right from the start. He didn't call us to the office at the same time—he called you first. You're the one he wants. And then you decided I had to be on the team too."

"Because you're the one with all the weird facts in your head," I said.

"That's the problem," said Seymour. "I know too much!"

"Seymour...," I began.

"Look," he interrupted, "forget about

what happened today. The truth is, I thought being on the *Quiz Kids* team was going to be a whole lot of fun, but it's not. Maria drives me nuts. Practices are boring—they're worse than sitting around in class. You be on the team. I'll be your personal trainer. It's the perfect solution."

It was also exactly what Mr. Phelps had wanted in the first place. Brother.

MEOW MEOW MEOW.

"What's wrong with T-Rex?" asked Seymour.

"He's hungry," I said. "Come in the house. I'll show you where he spent the afternoon. You'll be amazed!"

CHAPTER 8

"Hey, TJ. Come see this!"

Saturday morning I got up early, fiddled around with the old desk and watched TV for a while. When I heard Dad call from the front hall, I was pretty sure I knew what he'd found.

"Seems to me they've taken it right over," laughed Dad, pointing to the cats.

Alaska was sound asleep, curled into the folds of the fleece hoodie I'd lain across the top of the desk. T-Rex had jammed himself into one of the two drawers I'd left open. He looked totally pleased, and his tail hung over the edge like a furry bookmark...errr, desk-mark.

I thought about cat condo renovations

while we ate our fast-food breakfast. When we started up the hill toward the Jessop place, however, I could feel my stomach getting into a tighter and tighter knot. I *really* didn't want to have another run-in with Elizabeth Ann Jessop.

I tried telling myself she wouldn't be home. She was rich, so she'd be off playing polo somewhere. Her dog was rich, so he would be at the spa.

But when we got to the Jessops' house, there she was sitting on the front steps. Frooie came bounding to meet us like we were long-lost friends. Play it cool, I told myself. Keep your mouth shut and play it cool.

"Hey there, pup," said Dad, giving Frooie a friendly scratch behind his ears. "Eaten any good shoes lately?"

"No shoes," said Elizabeth. "But he got into a giant box of cornflakes first thing this morning. Mom made me vacuum the entire living room. Parts of it still crunch when you walk through."

Dad laughed.

"I'm supposed to tell you to just walk in,"

said Elizabeth. "They're in the kitchen."

Dad went inside without looking back. Elizabeth looked at me meaningfully. Except it wasn't really meaningful because I had no idea what it meant. My plan to play it cool began to teeter on the edge.

"Why are you looking at me like that?" I asked.

"I hope it's okay that I told them," she said.

"Told them what?" I asked.

"That he's your dad and that he owns the business too," said Elizabeth.

"Why wouldn't it be okay? It's the truth," I said. And then a very unpleasant thought hit me. "Unless it's because of the mess-up with tiling..."

To my surprise, Elizabeth began to smile and nod encouragingly.

"That's what it's about!" she said. "With the way your parents are making sure the tiling gets done properly, Mom figures she's finally found people she can trust to do a good job. Sometimes contractors rip people off like crazy up here. Mom's hoping

Rooms by Rita will do our kitchen next. Do you think your parents will agree?"

I'd been so convinced it was going to be something negative that it took a few seconds for my brain to really sort through the words. This wasn't negative—this was great. However, I still tried my best to play it cool.

"Well, they're pretty busy," I answered. "But I think they'll find a way to fit it in."

"I hope so," said Elizabeth. "It would be neat to see what design your mom comes up with. Can you believe Frooie broke into a box of cornflakes?"

Now she made it sound as if my parents' business and Frooie the cornflake-eating dog were somehow equal, which they *definitely* weren't in my mind, but I figured I could let it pass since I'd downplayed how pleased Mom and Dad would be. Besides, at the sound of his name, Frooie had begun to snuffle my fingers. Then he maneuvered the top of his head right under the palm of my hand. I pretty much had to pet him.

"He really is a nice dog," said Elizabeth,

"even if he does get into all kinds of trouble."

"T-Rex has been in trouble lately too," I said. "He's been getting trapped in weird places, like between doors and in the layers of floor under the living room. It's really strange to hear a cat running around under your feet."

"Did he get stuck?" asked Elizabeth. She actually sounded worried.

"We opened a tin of salmon," I said. "He got himself out."

"Food works for Frooie too," said Elizabeth. "I guess cats with weird names can get in as much trouble as dogs with weird names."

She brought out something from behind her back.

"Do you want to play Frisbee?" she asked. "I mean, since you don't have to supervise your dad?"

There was a lot of space in that big yard for throwing a Frisbee around. Frooie ran back and forth between us. Every once in a while he'd make an interception and then it would take us about ten minutes to get the Frisbee back again. Finally even Frooie was exhausted. We sat on the grass and watched him *glop glop glop* water out of the fishpond. A real fishpond. With real fish!

"I told the dog trainer about his tongue going backward," said Elizabeth. I guess I must have looked at her strangely then because her expression changed. "What?" she asked.

"It just seems weird...to have a dog trainer."

"It does?" she asked.

"A dog trainer and a huge house and a Mafia car and a yard the size of a baseball field."

"It's not that big," she said. She looked around and smiled. "Well, maybe about as big as the infield. I don't really notice, I guess. I've always lived here. It's my home."

She looked thoughtful for a moment and then glanced at me sideways.

"Mafia car. That's what Mom calls it too. She says people think lawyers are big-enough crooks without having a car that looks like it's paid for by the mob. It drives my stepdad crazy because he just really happens to like that kind of car."

A different type of vehicle was coming down the drive at the moment, however. It was Tony in his pickup truck.

"I'd better go," I said to Elizabeth. "I might be able to help."

Tony had just done the first two rows, with Dad doing most of the cuts and me passing things when needed, when I heard noises above us on the landing. Elizabeth and Frooie must have come through another door and up the back stairs to her bedroom. Now she was setting a stack of books on the top stair.

"Being out here is more fun than studying in my room," she called down. "And it's like watching one of those home makeover shows."

"Except we won't be finished in an hour," said Tony. "We're going to lay this out real pretty, though. A special work of art by Tony." Dad looked at me and winked. When Tony talks like that, things always turn out better than expected.

"I won't be finished in an hour either," said Elizabeth. She sighed as she looked at the books. "Oh well. Only one more week to go."

That meant she was studying for *Quiz Kids*. How could I not take a second look at the books beside her? Some looked like regular textbooks. Others were large and glossy—I recognized the expensive art books from the living room. That made me think of the paintings on the walls, the fancy piano and Elizabeth's mom being a professor. The kids in Fairview definitely had some advantages over the kids in our school.

When I looked back at the tiles being laid out before me, however, I saw what Tony meant. Bit by bit, a wonderful pattern of geometric intricacy was spreading out across the floor. Tiling isn't something that just anyone can do well. It's especially difficult in the tricky spots, like around the curving bottom of the stairs where the tiles have to be smaller at one end and larger at the other and grow gradually outward in a mathematical progression.

And Tony doesn't use pen-and-paper calculations either—he eyeballs it into place with intuition and experience.

That's when I really began to understand. There are a lot of different things to know in the world and a lot of different ways of knowing them. Academically, I probably wouldn't be able to touch Elizabeth and her teammates or the kids on my own team, but maybe—between Seymour's wild facts and some of the other things I knew—I could help out our school after all.

CHAPTER 9

One week to go until the *Quiz Kids* contest. That Monday at noon hour, Mr. Phelps called our team to the gym for a practice. There on the stage were the actual podiums, microphones and electronic buzzers that would be used the day of the contest. No one was more pleased than Maria.

"This is outstanding," she said. "You've brought in the equipment early from the TV station! It's going to be almost exactly like the competition itself, isn't it?"

Mr. Phelps nodded.

"The students at Fairview School do a lot of public speaking," he said. "We can't make up for that overnight, but at least we can treat this week like a dress rehearsal; it should help with the butterflies."

"Butterflies are right," said Seymour, standing at one of the podiums, looking out over our great giant gymnasium and imagining it packed with people. "Did I ever tell you about the time I was a shepherd in a Christmas pageant and got stage fright so badly I barfed all over my flock of sheep?"

"Another reason you shouldn't be on the team," said Maria.

"Definitely," said Seymour, climbing down from the stage.

Catchy theme music suddenly flooded the gym. We looked at Mr. Phelps. He was now wearing earphones and had stationed himself in front of a panel of switches and dials. An announcer's deep voice boomed out over the music.

"And now, from Riverside Elementary School, it's *The Quiz Kids TV Spectacular*!"

Practicing on the stage with podiums and microphones was definitely different than practicing with service bells in the science room. It felt a lot scarier, standing up on stage. Some teachers and students came in to watch us, so we actually had a small audience, and we even broke into two teams so we'd get used to working against people on the other side of the stage. It was a good experience. It also made all of us realize that these were our last five days before we experienced either the thrill of victory or the agony of defeat. And that's when I felt something else begin to happen.

Quiz Kids is a game, a competition. It's not real life. It's not going to determine whether someone is happy or sad. It's not really going to turn the kids from one school into winners and the kids from another school into losers. In the big scheme of things, *Quiz Kids* doesn't actually matter at all. I knew all that. And yet all of a sudden I could feel a great weight beginning to push down upon me. Pressure. Big-time. Part of me felt like I was walking very, very slowly on the bottom of the deepest part of the ocean, carrying a cannonball to weigh me down even further.

Seymour felt the pressure too. His reaction, however, was different from mine. Seymour went into maniac mode. Every moment he could find, he fed weird facts into my brain.

"Mosquitoes have heat sensors so they know where to bite to get your blood.

"There are three billion possible ways to play the first four moves in a chess game."

He fed me facts on the way to school, on the way home from school, in the middle of playing video games, over the phone last thing at night.

"There are one hundred lightning strikes for every second of every day all around the world.

"Tube worms never eat. They get all their food from germs that live in their bodies."

I tried my best to remember. Sometimes I made up wild stories in which tube worms were hit by one hundred strikes of lightning so that the germs inside them glowed warmly and attracted heat-sensing mosquitoes. Sometimes I made up sentences with clues in the first letter of each word. Other times I remembered facts just by thinking about how amazing they were.

"Vampire bats will die if they go two days without blood."

Two days! Two days isn't long at all. I knew vampire bats fed on blood, but I had no idea they'd die if they didn't eat for two days!

Seymour didn't stop with straight facts. The memory book said that being in the same location, and especially being around the same smells, helps people remember. At school, Seymour got permission for us to study on the stage itself. At home he wanted to spread dirty socks around the living room so it would smell the same as the gym. I didn't want to study around smelly socks!

And in the midst of all the studying, I still didn't tell my parents that I was going to be on *Quiz Kids*. I could *maybe* manage to stand up on stage with *Quiz Kids* and not fall apart, but I didn't want the extra pressure of having Mom and

Dad watch me. Every once in a while, however, I did share an amazing fact with them.

"Did you know frogs can use their eyeballs to eat?" I told them over supper Thursday night. "They can actually drop their eyeballs down below their eye sockets to help push food down their throat."

"Amazing," said Dad. "Strange. Bizarre. Slightly gross. But totally amazing."

"I have something amazing to share with you as well," said Mom. "Well, not quite as amazing as frogs and eyeballs. But it's amazing to me. And I had to do a lot of research. That desk in the hallway isn't just fifty or sixty years old. I'm almost certain that it's a true antique, over two hundred and fifty years old. And I've found an antique dealer who will give us a very good price."

"Congratulations!" said Dad. "Rooms *and* Antiques by Rita. "Then he looked at me and winked. "Mind you, the cats might not be as pleased."

"I was kind of thinking of turning it into a cat condo," I admitted. "But don't worry, they've got lots of other places to hang out. That's great, Mom."

"Thank you," said Mom. "Would it keep me in the cats' good books if I offered you carpet samples and the old wooden display stands from the shop? You could build them something from scratch. Pun intended."

"Even better," I said. "I'll give them their notice of eviction."

"We need to work out a few things though," said Mom. "The only time the dealer can stop by the house is this Saturday morning. I've got appointments with clients at the shop."

"Hmmm," said Dad. "Mr. G.'s still sick, and I'm helping Tony in exchange for the help he gave us last weekend. Plus I'm backup if Gladys's husband doesn't get back in time to take Gran and Gladys to the airport. And one of us should be at *Quiz Kids* to support Seymour..."

"I'll be there," I said quickly. "I can be at the house for the antique guy and still get to *Quiz Kids*. Seymour won't mind if you can't come—he'll give you the play-by-play later. He'll like that even better."

"Perfect," said Mom.

One day I'm going to remember that just when you think things are "perfect," that's when you need to worry most of all.

CHAPTER 10

On Saturday morning I lay in bed with a very strange sense of unreality. Today was the day I had to stand on stage and pretend I was a genius.

"TJ?" called Dad. "Can I come in?"

"Yup," I said.

"We'll go back to our regular junk-food breakfast next week, okay? And tell Seymour good luck. And I'll leave the bedroom door open so the cats can come and go."

"Yup," I said.

About half an hour later, Mom stopped at my door.

"TJ? Are you awake? There's three things I need to tell you."

"Awake," I said.

"Thing one—the people from Treasured Antiques should be coming to pick up the desk in the next hour or so."

"Desk," I said.

"Thing two—Gran's going to stop by for the suitcase on the way to the airport, but the clothes we're sending to Belize still need to be dried. Listen for the buzzer on the dryer and keep putting them through. Remember, there are two loads—one already in the dryer and one waiting to be dried."

"Clothes," I said.

"Thing three—tell Seymour good luck. Can you remember all that?"

"Seymour," I said.

Another half hour and the doorbell sounded a double-ring. I heard Seymour's voice in the front hall.

"TJ? TJ!"

T-Rex must have told him where I was. I heard them racing up the stairs together.

"Why are you still in bed?" demanded Seymour.

"I feel like I'm the wrong person in the wrong place at the wrong time," I told him.

"No big deal—I feel like that all the time," said Seymour. "Guess what? Mom's going to record the show so your parents can watch the tape while I tell them about it." He held up a clear plastic container. "And I brought you brain food for breakfast."

It looked like brains—gray and lumpy. Yuck.

I took as long as I could to shower and get dressed. I found Alaska nestled in my pile of clothes, and I spent a long time petting her. When I finally headed downstairs, she followed me. Seymour was in the kitchen, eating his way through a peanut-butter sandwich.

"Arachibutyrophobia—that's the fear of peanut butter sticking to the roof of your mouth," he announced. "I don't have it, but it's a great word."

I wondered if there was a word for how I felt about Seymour's brain food.

I ate cold cereal instead of the gray goop. Seymour talked about a guy who claimed that if we somehow squished all our molecules so that there was no space between the atoms and electrons and protons and all the other stuff that makes them, the entire human race would fit in a sugar cube. That got him babbling about even smaller particles called quarks that came in flavors named left, right, up, down, charmed and strange.

"They aren't going to ask that stuff," I said. "They're going to ask how many legs are on a spider."

"Dryer!" said Seymour.

At first I thought he was talking about either spiders or more flavors of quarks. He wasn't. The clothes dryer was buzzing. I'd almost forgotten about Gran and the clothes and her trip! I went into the laundry room and began to unload the dryer. One more load to go.

"Telephone!" said Seymour.

I left the dryer door open and went to answer the phone.

"Alaska!" said Seymour.

I went back to the laundry room. A tail was hanging out of the dryer. Alaska had climbed right inside to sleep on the warm clothes. It gave a whole new meaning to the term "fluff dry."

I lifted her out, shook cat hair from the T-shirts as I removed them, and put in the last load to dry.

"Telephone!" said Seymour.

Maria phoned twice to make sure we knew to be at school by noon. Rashid phoned to complain about Maria phoning. And then Gran phoned. Hurrah!

"The clothes are almost done," I told her. "Shall I put them in the suitcase?"

"Yes, please," she said. "And just leave it open. I've got some things to add when I get there. You'll have left the house by then, but I've got my key. It'll be a bit of a rush."

"I wish I could go with you to the airport to say good-bye," I told her.

"And I wish I could be at *Quiz Kids* **and** go to Belize," said Gran. "But we'll catch up on everything when I get back. The plane takes off about fifteen minutes before you go on stage. I'll shout 'go, TJ, go' as we fly over the school."

"Shout it quietly so you don't get kicked off the plane," I said.

"Right," laughed Gran. "Good luck, TJ."

"Have a great trip, Gran," I said.

After that, Amanda phoned to tell me that Elizabeth wanted to wish me good luck too. How did Elizabeth know I was on the team? And how did Amanda know Elizabeth? There wasn't time to find out. It was almost noon and the truck from Treasured Antiques had only just pulled up out front.

Luckily they took one look at the desk, decided it was genuine and carefully carried it to their truck. I threw the last of the clothes in the big suitcase, and Seymour and I raced to school, thinking everyone else would already be on stage.

Surprise—Mr. Phelps only wanted us there early for sound checks! Still two hours to go. Sound checks didn't take long at all, and then Mr. Phelps gave us strict instructions to wait in a classroom until we were called.

Waiting around in a room with a personal trainer and three other team members, including a girl named Maria who really, really, really wants to win, is a good way to destroy the nervous system. Seymour finally left because he said it gave him stage fright even though he wasn't going on stage.

At long last it was almost showtime, and we were called into the hallway to wait to go onstage.

"TJ?"

I turned in surprise. People had been arriving, but they'd come in at the other end of the school and gone straight to the gym. Now here was Dad beside me.

"I just saw Seymour. He sent me back here. Are you going onstage? I thought you were the alternate."

"I thought you were helping Tony," I said.

"I was, but we ran into a couple of snags, so..." Instead of finishing his sentence, Dad clammed right up.

"What?" I asked.

"Nothing," said Dad. "If you're here and

Seymour's out front watching, then you're on the team. I'll go and sit with Seymour and cheer you on."

"Wait," I said. "What's wrong? Why did you come?"

"It was nothing important," he said.

But there was something in Dad's face that said otherwise.

"You wouldn't have come if it wasn't important," I said. Suddenly I felt cold all over. "Is it...is it Gran? Did something happen to Gran's plane?"

Right away Dad shook his head.

"No," he said. "Gladys's husband phoned. They got away just fine a few minutes ago. They're in the air."

"Is it Mom?" I asked.

"No, TJ. She's fine."

"Tell me," I said.

"But you're about to go onstage..."

"Tell me," I said.

"Okay, but don't worry. She's probably just asleep somewhere. You know how she loves to sleep."

"Sleep? You mean Alaska?" I asked.

Dad grimaced.

"We ran into a snag on Tony's job, and I had to go back to the house to pick up some tools. I decided I better check the cats before I left. I found T-Rex, but I couldn't find Alaska. And then I saw the desk was gone..."

For a second my heart did a flip-flop. Alaska sound asleep in one of the desk drawers, rolling down the highway with Treasured Antiques. Who knows where she'd end up! But it was only for a second.

"It's okay," I said. "Alaska and T-Rex both watched out the window while the desk went down the front walk. I remember telling them that I'd build something even better. I'm sure of it."

"Perfect," said Dad. "She's in the house somewhere. Everything is okay."

"Just don't turn on the dryer without looking inside first," I said. "And she likes to sleep in the clean towels in the closet, but don't tell Mom. And there's some clothes I kicked under my bed kind of by accident. And..."

Someone touched me on the shoulder.

"Time to go, TJ," said Mr. Phelps.

The others were already standing at the doors to the music room.

"I'll be out in the audience," said Dad. "Everything's fine."

Elizabeth was standing at the other door to the music room with her team. She gave Amanda and me a big wave. Maria looked at both of us suspiciously.

"Focus," she said.

Amanda took a deep breath. Rashid went into quiet mode, but with a smile that held a hint of anticipation...like Alaska when she's about to pounce on a spider.

As for me, a funny little refrain began to play in the back of my brain. *Something's wrong. Something's wrong. Something's wrong.*

I checked my fly. Nope. That wasn't it.

The music began to blare.

"And now...from Riverside Elementary School...it's *The Quiz Kids TV Spectacular!*"

CHAPTER 11

Physicists have all sorts of theories about time, but I don't know if any of them allow for how time becomes completely unpredictable when hundreds and hundreds of faces and three separate TV cameras are all staring at you.

Out onto the stage we went. It seemed to take forever to reach my spot at the podiums. It seemed to take an eternity to get through the introductions. Even the first question, which was multiple choice, just as we'd always practiced, seemed to come out slow, slow, slow.

"The process by which plants convert sunlight to food is known as: a) sublimation, b) res—"

Bzzt.

It was way too easy of course. Both teams hit the buzzer at almost the same time, but it was Amanda's light that lit up.

"Photosynthesis."

"Correct. The term that describes the process by which water changes from a liquid to a gas is known as a) oxidization, b) fre—"

Bzzt.

This time it was Fairview's light, and their captain answered correctly. "Evaporation."

After that, questions came steadily, and time began to fly. Riverside. Fairview. Riverside. Fairview. Name the country with the largest population. Name the type of rock that is formed in layers. I knew some of the answers, but I couldn't ring in nearly fast enough. The action had been kicked up a notch. Things were moving really fast. I felt like I was being left in the dust and my confidence was doing a total nosedive. *Ask about oceans. Ask about lightning. Ask about sweating hippos.*

It didn't happen. And all the time, softly but persistently, the refrain kept playing in the back of my brain: *Something's wrong. Something's wrong. Something's wrong.*

We were halfway through individual questions.

"TJ, your question is: what two tributaries of similar name contribute to the River Nile?"

I knew it was in Egypt. I knew it flooded. I knew it was called the longest river in the world. I had no idea at all what its tributaries were.

"Nile One and Nile Two?"

It was so obviously a guess that the moderator smiled.

"Incorrect." He turned to the other team. "Anyone on Fairview?"

"The Blue Nile and the White Nile," said a kid named Garrison.

Not fair! They'd probably all been to Egypt on a class trip! Okay, even I knew their school didn't have *that* much money. But for half a second it made me feel better. I needed to feel better!

More questions. Riverside. Fairview. Riverside. Fairview.

Something's wrong. Something's wrong. Something's wrong.

"We now pause for a station break."

We all stepped back from the microphones. Mr. Phelps brought us water and told us we were doing just fine.

"It's definitely a stronger competition than last year." Talk about being comfortable on stage—Elizabeth Jessop had walked in front of everyone to talk to us!

"Garrison said we'd beat you before the first break. I told him he was overconfident," she continued. "Ooops...I'm getting daggers sent my way."

She scurried back to her side.

"Beaten before the first break!" said Rashid. "We're practically tied with them!"

"We would be tied if I hadn't blown my question," I said.

"I didn't know the answer," said Amanda.

"I did," said Maria.

"Teams...ten seconds and counting."

"Focus," said Maria.

Focusing didn't seem to be doing me a whole lot of good. I looked out into the audience and happened to see Seymour. He gave me the thumbs-up sign. I had to keep trying.

The questions began again and the score remained tied, with correct answers splitting evenly again. Fairview. Riverside. Fairview. Riverside.

"The subject is words and definitions," said the moderator. "Name the term that describes a word that reads the same forward and backward."

"Evil olive," answered Garrison.

His answer came so fast that you knew he'd had it ready just in case. Being that well prepared, however, had worked against him. He hadn't listened carefully enough to the question.

"Incorrect," said the moderator. "Riverside?"

"A palindrome," said Rashid.

We'd regained some ground. I didn't know if it was enough to make up for the points I'd missed, but it would help.

"Name the plural of ox."

"Oxen," answered Elizabeth.

"Name a homophone that means both a carpenter's tool and an area of flat land."

Bzzt.

All of a sudden everyone was looking at me. Why were they looking at me? Why was my hand on the buzzer? I didn't know what a homophone was. I'd only rung in because there was a word in my head that fit the definitions.

"TJ?" asked the moderator.

"A plane and a plain," I said. "Except they're spelled differently."

"Correct," said the moderator.

I'd got one. I'd actually got one. All on my own. Just keep trying, I told myself, just keep trying. Now the subject was math. I missed two questions by hesitating the slightest fraction of a second. The third time I didn't hesitate.

"One hundred and one," I answered. Don't ask me how I knew that 101 was the first prime number after one hundred, but I did.

The questions kept coming. I kept trying, but I could tell that my brain was beginning to zone out. Amanda, Rashid and Maria, however, just kept going. Answer for answer, they matched the Fairview team right up until the very last section.

"Congratulations, both teams," said the moderator. "A hard-fought battle, and the score is tied. And now it's time for the final bonus round...right after this break."

This time, Elizabeth stayed with her own team. They were discussing something with an intensity that could be felt even on our side of the stage.

"Don't worry about the huddle over there," said Mr. Phelps. "It's part of their strategy. They're trying to psych you out."

It was working. Maria was biting her lip. Rashid had grown very solemn. Only Amanda seemed to be maintaining her cool.

"Teams...ten seconds."

Everyone got into position.

"Welcome back to *Quiz Kids,* where the score is tied, and we are entering the final portion of the competition," said the moderator. "These are open questions. Either team may answer. The team that answers correctly will then have the opportunity for bonus points."

"True or false. Marsupials are mammals."

Bzzt.

The buzzer rang just as the moderator began the first "m" in the word "mammals." The timing was perfect. Fairview had been able to hear the entire question without leaving us even the tiniest split second to sneak in before them.

"True," answered Garrison. Self-confidence radiated from him like a heat wave.

"The bonus opportunity goes to Fairview," said the moderator. "Name five marsupials for ten bonus points each."

Fairview was allowed a five-second huddle.

"Opossums," came the answer. "Kangaroos, wallabies, koalas and... and...duck-billed platypus."

"Four correct answers," said the moderator. "Duck-billed platypus is incorrect. Fairview, you are now in the lead. Riverside, there is still room for you to tie or win. Again, a true-or-false question. Bats..."

Bzzt!

Amanda had hit the buzzer faster than a fly changing direction.

There was complete silence in the auditorium. Everyone thought Amanda had jumped the gun. She'd rung in so fast we didn't even know the question.

Everyone thought that was the case, that is, except Seymour. Out in the audience, Seymour was smiling. It was exactly what he would have done. As far as Seymour was concerned it was one of those school-type questions that you could see coming a mile away. And Amanda knew it too.

"False," said Amanda. And then just for good measure she added, "The statement 'bats are blind' is false."

The moderator let the moment of suspense linger as long as possible.

"Correct," he said at last. "And now, for a possible win, for ten points each, name five categories of food eaten by bats."

Our turn to huddle. Insects. Fruit. Nectar. Blood. One more. One more.

Out in the audience, Seymour closed his eyes and placed his spread fingers carefully on either side of his temples. He was doing the Vulcan Mind Meld. He knew the answer. With all the babbling he'd done at me, I must know the answer too. Somewhere in my brain I must know it...but where? If only he'd acted it out!

And then all of a sudden I saw it. He *had* acted it out, flapping his elbows like skinny little bat wings and doing a clawing thing with his hands as he skimmed low over the surface of the carpet to pick up his dinner. I remembered because Alaska had looked at him like he was crazy from where she was sniffing the suitcase Mom had left open to air on the sofa. I'd been wondering if Alaska would climb inside to sleep, but I guess an empty suitcase wasn't soft enough for her. Oh no! I could feel myself going cold all over. The suit-case hadn't been empty this afternoon. I'd filled it myself. And the cat who loved to burrow and fall asleep had watched me...Oh no—this was awful!

Amanda had already started giving our answer.

"Insects, fruit, nectar, blood and... and..."

"Fish!" I shouted. "And Alaska's on her way to Belize!"

The siren rang to end the contest as I raced from the stage to explain things to Dad.

CHAPTER 12

Sunday morning at nine o'clock there isn't a lot happening at our small local airport. Dad, Mom, Seymour and I had already been there for an hour, though, just in case.

"We found her, TJ!" Gran had called from the huge international airport late the previous afternoon. "She's okay."

An open suitcase and a fluffy bed of warm, soft clothes—how could Alaska resist? Just like Dad, Gran had been in a hurry, quickly putting her own bag of clothing and notebooks on top and closing the lid. Gladys's husband hadn't thought twice about how much the suitcase weighed when he carried it to the car.

The two hours right after *Quiz Kids*—with Dad phoning the airlines and the baggage people and the neighbor's niece's best friend's father and trying to reach Gran and waiting to hear back from her—were the hardest hours I've ever spent.

"She'll be fine," Seymour had kept reassuring me. "A cat once flew in its owner's luggage from Paris to Montreal and it survived just fine. They opened the suitcase at a Montreal hotel and—surprise!—there was the cat. It's true. I've got the newspaper clipping."

Please be fine. Please be fine. Please be fine.

And then Gran had phoned with the good news.

"Is she really okay?" I asked.

"Yes," said Gran. "We have her wrapped in a blanket and she's purring. You can listen."

I listened. Even long distance it sounded like purring.

"Did you hear her?"

"I did! I heard her."

"We're already working on a plan to get her back to you," said Gran.

Six Degrees of Separation, or at least four degrees, was coming to the rescue. The best friend's father's sister had offered to help. She wasn't traveling, but she'd been at the airport and she liked cats. A proper traveling case, a trip to the vet to be extra sure all was well, a good home overnight, and this morning Alaska was flying home under the seat of a cat-loving flight attendant—which is first class for a cat.

"What time is it?" I asked Seymour. We were standing at the windows, hoping to see the plane come in.

"One minute later than the last time you asked," he said. "And I sure hope that's Amanda, her mom and what's-her-name who owns the dog walking toward us because you could definitely use some distraction."

What were they doing here?

"We decided it was an occasion worth celebrating," said Amanda, handing me a pouch of kitty treats.

"Don't tell Frooie or he'll be jealous," said Elizabeth, handing me a tin of gourmet cat food.

"I don't get it," I said. "How do you two know each other?"

"We're in the same swim club," said Amanda. "Aqua Racers includes kids from all over, including a lot of kids from Fairview. That's how I knew about them being so competitive. Didn't you know?"

"And when Mrs. Jessop and I were visiting at one of the swim meets, I learned she wanted to do some renovations. I told her about Rooms by Rita, which I hear has turned out well for everyone," said Amanda's mom. "Are your folks here, TJ? I need them for one more little job before they get too busy up in Fairview."

As Mrs. Baker crossed to where Mom and Dad were sitting, two tourists with huge suitcases came rolling by. Amanda looked at the luggage and shook her head.

"I still can't believe it," she said. "Alaska asleep in a suitcase."

"It's a good thing you figured it out before they left the country," said Elizabeth.

"There would have been vaccinations and quarantine time and everything else before she could come back in."

"I think they X-ray luggage or something on international flights," said Seymour. "I guess maybe a cat would show up. Or not. Actually, I don't know."

"Good grief...something odd that you don't know," said Amanda.

"I'll work on it," said Seymour.

"I wish I knew where to look to see the plane arrive," I said.

"I'll find out," said Elizabeth.

She headed off toward one of the airline counters. Seymour followed her. Amanda looked at me sideways.

"I think Elizabeth likes you," she said.

"She can't like me," I said. "I live in a regular house and I ride around in a beat-up old truck and my cats don't have a pedigree or a cat trainer."

"Some kids at Fairview care about things like that, but Elizabeth doesn't, not really," said Amanda. "I mean, sometimes she forgets that not everybody has heaps of money—you should have seen the price of the swim suits she thought the team should get—but once I told her that I could either eat that month or have a new swim suit, she began to get the idea. And besides...her dog's as goofy as your cats."

Elizabeth and Seymour were hurrying toward the windows at the far end of the terminal.

"We talked to the flight attendant for the next flight," said Seymour. "She says we'll be able to see Alaska's plane any minute now, coming in from the south."

The flight attendant came to join us, pointing out the exact spot above the horizon.

There. A flash of silver in the morning sun. I felt myself blinking hard like some stupid little kid. I couldn't help it. It had been awful getting home last night and not seeing her furry face in the window. The house had been empty, empty, empty. That shining dot meant Alaska was coming home.

Elizabeth turned just in time to see me swallow hard. She didn't say anything but

I could tell she understood. She would have felt the same way about Frooie, even though he was way too big to fit in a suitcase.

I kept my eye on the plane—landing, taxiing, unloading—until finally I saw the crate being carried into the terminal. I expected to hear her then—T-Rex would have been howling his head off—but all was quiet as they handed me the crate.

"Is she okay?" asked Seymour.

I opened the door and looked inside. Two green eyes looked at me sleepily. I slipped my hand inside. Lick. Lick. Lick. A rough tongue was saying hello to my hand. Alaska was just fine.

Elizabeth and Amanda didn't come home with us. I didn't ask them to. I'm not sure if I want some girl to like me. But I did tell Elizabeth that if she and Frooie were still going to be at the dog show the next month, Seymour and I would drop by and say hi. Elizabeth said she'd watch for us.

There were important things to do when we got back to our house, things like feeding both cats lots of treats and petting them and playing with them and phoning people to thank them and leaving a message for Gran to let her know everything was okay.

"An adventure with a happy ending—the very best kind," said Mom, settling down on the couch. "And now that it has ended happily, I'm wondering if anyone has any idea about something interesting to watch on TV. Something a mother might like to watch? A mother who didn't get a chance to see her son on TV helping his team win a *Quiz Kids* contest?"

"Showtime!" said Seymour, rummaging in his backpack.

As Seymour slipped the tape into the machine, Dad settled into his favorite chair. T-Rex stretched out long and relaxed on the rug. I picked up Alaska and set her on top of me, where she promptly fell asleep as the theme music began to play.

I remembered the moment in Mr. Phelps's office when he'd first asked me to be on the team. It felt like I'd come miles and miles and miles since then. Frankly, I felt totally exhausted.

My name is TJ Barnes. The capital of Peru is Lima. The Wright brothers flew the first airplane in 1902. And you'd need to buy seven dozen hot dogs to feed forty-two players two hot dogs each.

But I never want to be on another *Quiz Kids TV Spectacular* for as long as I live.

Some of the books where Seymour found his strange and amazing facts

Berger, Melvin and Gilda. *Fish Sleep But Don't Shut Their Eyes.* Scholastic, 2004.

Berger, Melvin and Gilda. *Hurricanes Have Eyes But Can't See.* Scholastic, 2004.

Berger, Melvin and Gilda. *You're Tall in the Morning But Shorter at Night.* Scholastic, 2004.

Funston, Sylvia. *Who Are You?* Maple Tree Press, 2004.

Funston, Sylvia and Jay Ingram. *A Kid's Guide to the Brain.* Greey De Pencier Books, 1994.

Imes, Rick. *Incredible Bugs.* Macmillan, 1997.

Maynard, Christopher. *Amazing Animal Facts.* Stoddart, 1993.

Romanek, Trudee. *Squirt.* Kids Can Press, 2006.

Settel, Joanne. *Exploding Ants.* Atheneum, 1999.

Thomas, Lyn. *What? What? What?* Maple Tree Press, 2003.

Treays, Rebecca. *Understanding Your Brain.* Usborne, 1995.

Hazel Hutchins lives in the mountain town of Canmore, Alberta. Author of forty children's titles, she has won numerous awards and enjoys visiting schools and libraries across Canada when she isn't writing.

Other books about
TJ, Seymour and the cats:

TJ and the Cats
TJ and the Haunted House
TJ and the Rockets
TJ and the Sports Fanatic